I SURVIVED

THE BATTLE OF GETTYSBURG, 1863

I SURVIVED

THE SINKING OF THE *TITANIC*, 1912

THE SHARK ATTACKS OF 1916

HURRICANE KATRINA, 2005

THE BOMBING OF PEARL HARBOR, 1941

THE SAN FRANCISCO EARTHQUAKE, 1906

THE ATTACKS OF SEPTEMBER 11, 2001

THE BATTLE OF GETTYSBURG, 1863

I SURVIVED

THE BATTLE OF GETTYSBURG, 1863

by Lauren Tarshis

illustrated by Scott Dawson

Scholastic Inc.

TO KAREN TARSHIS, MY BEAUTIFUL MOM

ISBN 978-0-545-45936-5

12 11 10 9 8 7 6   13 14 15 16 17 18/0

Printed in the U.S.A.   40
First printing, January 2013
Designed by Tim Hall

CHAPTER 1

JULY 2, 1863
A BATTLEFIELD IN GETTYSBURG,
PENNSYLVANIA

It was the battle of Gettysburg, the biggest and bloodiest of the Civil War.

Mighty armies from the United States' North and South were fighting to the death. Cannons shook the ground and set the sky on fire. Bullets flew through the air like deadly raindrops.

And in the middle of it all stood an eleven-year-old boy named Thomas.

Just three weeks before, Thomas had been a slave living on a farm in Virginia. And now he was on this battlefield in Pennsylvania, trying to help the Northern soldiers, who were fighting so he could be free.

Thomas had come to bring the men more ammunition for their rifles. He had to get away from here. He needed to get back to his little sister, who was waiting where it was safe.

But then a huge cannonball came sailing through the air. It crashed into an ammunition wagon.

Kaboom!

Flames shot up. Tree branches turned into torches. Razor-sharp strips of metal and nails flew through the air, stabbing Thomas in the leg and cutting his forehead. He dove for cover, rolling down a slippery hill. Gun smoke filled the air, choking him, blinding him. He had to get away!

He staggered across a field, coughing and

gagging. Blood spilled into his eyes from the gash on his forehead and gushed from the cut on his leg.

And through the blood and smoke was a terrifying sight: hundreds of rebel soldiers charging across the meadow, their rifles pointed right at him.

Boom!

Boom!

Boom!

Thomas ran, but not fast enough.

He turned and saw a rebel soldier running straight for him. The soldier's eyes were red with fury. His face was twisted into a crazed grin.

He aimed his rifle at Thomas.

No! Thomas couldn't die here!

Boom!

Thomas's chest seemed to shatter like glass.

He jerked back, and fell onto the blood-soaked grass.

CHAPTER 2

THREE WEEKS EARLIER
LATE AFTERNOON
KNOX'S FARM, OAK RIDGE, VIRGINIA

Thomas crept slowly toward the squirrel. It was fat and would make a fine supper. Just thinking about it made his stomach rumble. Times were tough on the farm. His owner, Mr. Knox, could barely feed his horses — or his slaves.

Thomas was just about to snare the squirrel when his little sister's voice sang out.

"Thomas!"

The squirrel darted away.

Thomas turned toward Birdie, fuming. She was only five years old, but she knew better than to yell when he was trying to hunt!

But then there she was, with her crooked grin and twiggy legs, rushing toward him. His heart turned to mush.

"Look what I caught!" she said proudly, holding out her cupped hands.

Inside was a little green snake, covered with mud.

"Isn't it beautiful?" she said.

Thomas had to smile.

That was Birdie: Give her a grimy little snake, and she'd see a butterfly.

Birdie held up her hands and looked at the baby snake, putting her face so close Thomas thought she might kiss it.

"All right," she said to the snake. "I'm going to let you go now."

She crouched down and released it onto the dirt.

5

They watched as the creature streaked away, disappearing into the shadows of the forest.

Thomas wondered: Would he and Birdie ever be as free as that snake?

They'd been born slaves on this farm. Their mama had died here when Birdie was a baby. And two summers ago their cousin Clem had been sold away to a plantation down in Mississippi, where slaves were worked half to death.

Clem was only seventeen at the time, but he'd been almost like a father to them after Mama died. He'd watched over them, cared for them, protected them.

And he'd taught Thomas about freedom.

He said that not far from here, in the states up north, slavery was illegal. People there believed it was evil. Clem told stories about slaves who'd run away from their owners. They'd followed the North Star, the brightest star in the sky. They'd traveled for days and days and made it to freedom. They were brave enough to run through dark forests and snake-filled swamps. They were clever enough to outsmart the slave catchers, who tracked them with ferocious dogs that could smell them from miles away.

"But then they make it to freedom, just like we will one day," Clem would say, his eyes flashing like tiny torches. "One day we will *run*."

He'd close his eyes.

"Picture it, Thomas," he'd say. "Picture it in your mind. Can't you see us? Can't you see us all together?"

And Thomas *could* see it, bright pictures that filled his mind and gave him a flickering feeling of hope in his heart.

But then Clem was taken, and those pictures went dark.

Just thinking about Clem gave Thomas a searing pain, even worse than the lash of Mr. Knox's whip. Now the only picture in his mind was one of Clem being dragged away in chains.

"Are you sad, Thomas?" Birdie said, looking up at him.

He put his hand on her head. "How could I be sad with you here with me?" he said.

With Clem gone, it was up to Thomas to make Birdie feel safe.

"I'm just thinking about how to catch us a nice supper," he said.

He sent Birdie back to their shack to weed their garden. But just a few minutes later she was back. She was breathing hard, her eyes wide and scared.

Was she hurt?

"Those men are here," she whispered, grabbing Thomas's hand.

"What men?" Thomas said.

Hardly anyone came to the farm anymore. Mrs. Knox was dead. Mr. Knox's two sons were gone, fighting in the war.

"Those bad men," Birdie said. "The ones who took Clem."

Thomas's heart cracked open.

"I heard them talking," Birdie said, her words choked by tears. "They've come for *you*!"

Thomas heard voices from across the field; Mr. Knox calling for him.

"Boy!" Mr. Knox was yelling. "I need you now!"

Thomas stood there, frozen.

He heard Clem's voice in his mind.

Run!

Thomas grabbed Birdie.

And like that little snake, Thomas and Birdie disappeared into the shadowy forest.

CHAPTER 3

Thomas carried Birdie on his back, walking deeper and deeper into the woods.

It got dark, and he found the North Star.

The night sounds rose up — the hoots of owls and the shimmer of crickets. Animals shrieked and howled. His back ached from carrying Birdie, his muscles twisting into knots of pain.

But he didn't stop. They needed to get as far as they could from the farm.

Because soon the slave catchers would be after them.

Clem had told Thomas about those men, who chased down runaway slaves and collected rewards for returning them to their owners. Their dogs were vicious and as big as mules. Thomas could practically smell the stink of their hot breath, hear their snapping jaws, and feel their teeth ripping into his flesh.

The night got darker and darker. Danger seemed to be everywhere — looming in the trees, glowing in the eyes of the night creatures peering from bushes. Twice, Thomas stopped, too terrified to take another step.

They should go back!

He could lie to Mr. Knox, swear they'd gotten lost chasing rabbits. But he knew what happened to runaways — they'd be whipped, or worse.

Thomas kept going.

Finally the sun started to rise.

The shadows disappeared and the birds started singing.

In the distance, Thomas saw fields and farmhouses.

It was too dangerous to walk through a town during the day. They'd find a place to hide and wait until dark. Birdie was so tired. Thomas brought her down to a stream and helped her wash up. Just up the bank was a fallen tree with some soft ground on one side and a leafy bush on the other — a perfect hiding spot. He sat down and Birdie curled up next to him.

Within a minute she was fast asleep. And Thomas dozed, too.

He didn't sleep long, and he woke up thirsty.

He went down to the stream for a drink. He washed the dust from his face and soaked his battered feet. For a few seconds he let himself believe that he and Birdie were on an adventure together, that maybe Clem was even waiting for him just up the hill.

But then there were new sounds:

Running footsteps, snapping twigs, the pounding of horses' hooves.

Thomas hurried back up the bank, diving through the bushes and into the dirt next to Birdie.

"We see you there!" a man's voice bellowed.

The slave catchers!

A rifle clicked.

"Come out now," another voice snarled. "Or we'll shoot you."

CHAPTER 4

Birdie looked at Thomas, too terrified to even cry.

"They won't hurt us, Birdie," Thomas whispered, praying this was true, trying to keep his voice steady.

But his entire body was trembling.

He heard the sound of stirrups clinking, of boots on the ground.

The men were coming!

Thomas stood up and was about to shout, "Don't shoot us!"

But then he caught a glimpse of the men.

There were two, and they weren't facing Thomas and Birdie. Their rifles were aimed up into a tree. And they were wearing gray uniforms, the same as Mr. Knox's sons had worn when they went off to war.

Thomas quickly ducked back down.

Something was strange.

He turned to Birdie and put his finger on his lips. Then he peeped up again, trying to get a better look.

There were no dogs anywhere.

Was it possible . . . ?

"We see you up there!" one of the men called up into the tree. "Get down now or we'll blow you to pieces!"

They were not slave catchers. They were soldiers.

They weren't looking for Thomas and Birdie!

But who were they chasing?

Thomas studied the men. One of them was very tall, with a straggly beard. The other was skinny with a bushy brown mustache.

There was a rustling in the tree the men stood

beside. A boot appeared, and then someone dropped onto the ground.

A man. He looked to be around Clem's age.

He wasn't tall, but he looked powerful. His face was smudged with dirt, and his tangled brown hair was matted with leaves. He was wearing a uniform, too, a dark blue one. It was torn and soaked in sweat. His expression was fierce as he rose slowly to his feet.

Thomas guessed he was a Yankee — a soldier fighting for the North.

Thomas didn't know much about the war — just that the North and South were fighting against each other. He had no idea why.

Suddenly Birdie started to whimper.

Thomas ducked down, pulling her to him.

Didn't she know to stay quiet?!

And then he saw what Birdie was whimpering about: The biggest skunk he'd ever seen was only a few feet from them, nosing around in the leaves. It didn't seem to notice Thomas and Birdie . . . yet.

He held Birdie tight to his chest. He couldn't worry about the skunk now.

He craned his neck so he could keep an eye on the soldiers. He wished they'd just do their business and get out of here.

"You'll be sorry you ever came here, boy!" growled the tall Southern soldier. He took a pistol from his belt. And as quick as a snakebite, he smashed it into the blue soldier's face. There was a sickening cracking sound. The blue soldier fell to his knees, blood spurting from his nose.

"What are you doing?!" the other gray soldier yelled. "Our orders are to bring back prisoners, not beat them to death!"

"Shut up!" the tall man bellowed, his voice so vicious that the other man backed off.

Thomas's heart pounded. He hugged Birdie closer, putting his hands over her ears so she wouldn't hear the curses and cries.

The tall man stepped up and kicked the blue soldier, who doubled over, groaning in pain. Then the fallen man looked up, and somehow, his desperate eyes found Thomas, peering through the tangle of leaves.

Thomas felt a strange jolt.

That look: He'd seen it before.

It was the same look Clem had had when the men took him away.

The tall man placed the barrel of his pistol at the side of the blue soldier's head.

"You're gone, Yankee," he said, clicking back the hammer.

CHAPTER 5

Thomas's mind was swirling.

He looked at the skunk. And without really thinking, he lunged for it, grabbing it by the tail.

Hissssssss!

It reared around, snapping its little jaws. Its sharp teeth almost clamped down on Thomas's cheek.

"Hey!" he called.

The tall man looked over at Thomas, his eyes flashing with surprise, and then fury.

And then, with all of his might, Thomas hurled the skunk toward the men.

Thud.

It landed right in front of one of the horses.

There was a split second of silence.

And then an explosion of noise — screeching horses, shouting men, the shriek of the skunk.

"Stay down!" he whispered to Birdie.

But Thomas only kneeled, watching the scene of panic.

The horses reared up, their heads twisting in fear as the air filled with the rotten smell.

The men, coughing and gagging, struggled to calm the horses. They grabbed for the reins, dodging the horses' flying hooves.

But the horses broke free and bolted into the woods at full speed.

The men shouted to each other.

"Get the horses!"

"Hurry!"

"Just leave him!"

They thundered into the woods after their animals.

Thomas sat there for a few seconds, stunned and choking in the sour cloud.

Then he came to his senses. He and Birdie had to get out of there!

Those men could be back any second!

"Come on, Birdie!" he said, ready to run.

But then voices rang out in the distance.

More soldiers!

"Corporal Green!" a voice boomed. "Green! Where are you?"

A group of five blue soldiers hurried over, led by a man with a thick silver beard. They huddled around the injured man.

"It was the rebels, Captain Campbell," the bloodied soldier — Corporal Green — rasped. "They were on horseback . . . cavalry, I think. They attacked me, sir, back near our camp, when I was getting some firewood. They chased me here. They were halfway to killing me."

"I hear reports that there could be hundreds of rebel cavalry around here," the captain said. "Let's get back to camp, before this stink kills us all!"

The men helped Corporal Green to his feet.

"Can you walk?" said the captain.

"Yes, sir . . . but wait."

The corporal turned and looked over to where Thomas and Birdie were hiding.

Thomas huddled against the fallen tree, his heart pounding.

But suddenly six sets of curious eyes were looking down at Thomas and Birdie.

Birdie smiled at them, and Thomas saw their eyes soften.

And then Corporal Green held out his hand to Thomas.

"I'm Henry," he said, shaking Thomas's hand. "Captain," Henry said, turning, "meet the boy who saved my life."

CHAPTER 6

```
TWO WEEKS LATER
5:30 A.M.
UNION ARMY CAMP,
MIDDLEBURG, VIRGINIA
```

The bugle blared reveille, and Thomas sat up
with a start.

All around him he could hear the sounds of
sleepy men, groaning and cussing at the bugler.

Birdie was curled up next to him. She snuffled,
but didn't wake up. In her hands was a little doll

Henry had made for her, a tattered sock stuffed with straw, with two cracked buttons as eyes. From the way Birdie clutched it to her heart, you'd think it was made of gold.

Thomas peeked his head out of the tent and looked around the army camp, which stretched out across a huge field. There were hundreds of tents, crammed together in rows. A few early-rising soldiers stood groggily and shaved in front of mirrors hung from tree branches.

There were more than six hundred men here, Henry had explained, just one regiment of the huge Union army. They'd been camped here for three months, waiting for their next big battle with the rebel soldiers of the South.

At first, Thomas was sure he and Birdie wouldn't be allowed to stay here.

But the story of Thomas and the skunk had swept through the camp. Soldiers came up to Thomas, smiled at him, and patted him on the back, said that the Union army should start shooting skunks out of their cannons. And soon enough, Thomas felt almost like he and Birdie belonged there. They got their own tent. There was plenty of food, and Birdie had never been happier. She had the run of the camp and spent most of her days helping two older soldiers, Lester and Homer, with the supply wagons.

Les even made her a new dress, out of an old flour sack.

For the first time in Thomas's life, his ears didn't ring with the sound of Mr. Knox shouting, "Boy! You get here now!" He didn't drop to sleep at night aching from his head to his toes. He woke up in the morning looking forward to the day — to helping the men with their chores, listening to their stories, and watching them practice their battle formations and shooting.

And best of all, there was Henry, who'd barely let Thomas out of his sight since that day in the woods. "You know how it works," Henry had told Thomas. "You save a man's life, you're stuck with him forever."

He really did remind Thomas of Clem, the

way his voice rose up when he told stories about the children he taught in his Vermont school-house, his patient way of listening when Thomas told him about his life with Mr. Knox, the feeling Thomas got when they were together, that he and Birdie were safe.

Thomas had just climbed out of his tent when Henry appeared.

"Morning, soldier," the corporal said.

Birdie's head popped out of the tent. When she saw Henry standing there she leaped up and threw her arms around him.

"I love my doll!" she said, beaming up at him.

"No doll could ever be as pretty as you, Birdie," Henry said, kneeling down. "Les and Homer are looking for you. Can you ask them to put an extra biscuit aside for me?"

She nodded happily and scampered off toward the supply wagons, chattering hellos to every soldier she passed. Thomas noticed that even the weariest men looked up and smiled when Birdie breezed by, their faces lighting up as though Birdie herself were a bright candle.

Henry turned to Thomas, his face serious.

"We've gotten our orders," Henry said. "We're to march out today."

Thomas's heart sank.

The men were leaving? What would happen to him and Birdie?

Henry seemed to read Thomas's thoughts.

"Of course you and Birdie are coming with us," he said.

"I'm glad about that," Thomas said, relief washing over him.

"You won't be when we get out into that heat," Henry said with a little smile. "It's going to be brutal. Two days, I'd say."

"Where are we heading?" Thomas said.

"We're marching to Pennsylvania," Henry said. "The town's called Gettysburg."

Henry squinted into the distance.

"It seems like we're in for a big battle."

CHAPTER 7

The men scrambled to fold up their tents, pack up their knapsacks, and fill their canteens at the stream. Already they were grumbling about the heat. Birdie skipped around as if she was getting ready to go to a party.

Thomas helped Les ready the horses for the trip, keeping his ears pricked up as he worked. A person learned by listening; that's what Clem always said. Sure enough, Thomas had learned more in the past two weeks than he'd learned in the past two years.

The men were always talking about their families and their sweethearts, their hometowns and their plans for getting back home. And, of course, they talked about the war.

It turned out what Clem had said was right: People in the North *did* think slavery was evil. It had been illegal in the North for years. Now President Lincoln wanted to end slavery everywhere in America.

Except the people in the South didn't care what President Lincoln thought. They wanted to keep their slaves. Eleven Southern states were already trying to break away from the United States to start their own country.

A country with slavery.

Here's what Thomas had figured out: If the North won the war, the states would stay together, and slavery would be gone forever.

And if the South won?

Thomas tried not to think about that.

But listening to the men each night, it was hard not to worry. The North had more soldiers, and better weapons and uniforms. But the rebel fighters were fierce, even though some fought barefoot, with rickety guns that could barely shoot. They had a ferocious battle cry — the rebel yell — that they screamed out when they were charging. "It sounds like you're being attacked by a pack of wild beasts," Henry had told him. "The sound will chill you right to your bones."

And now Thomas could see how worried the men looked as they packed up the camp. Thomas overheard Les and Homer talking behind the supply wagons. He didn't mean to spy, but they were talking in loud voices.

"This is going to be another Fredericksburg," Lester said. "I can feel it!"

"Don't say that, Les! Don't even think it!" Homer said.

Later, Thomas asked Henry about what he'd heard.

Henry didn't answer right away.

"Fredericksburg was a big battle we fought," he said. "Back in December."

"What happened there?"

Henry looked into his knapsack, rummaging around, as though he might find the answer folded up with his blanket.

But then he dropped his pack and sat down. He patted the grass next to him, and Thomas sat, too.

Henry's face got a faraway look.

And then, in a low voice, Henry told the story of that day.

CHAPTER 8

"We were told it was to be a surprise attack," Henry began. "Tens of thousands of Union troops were to march to a town in Virginia — Fredericksburg. We would attack the rebels, take the town, and then march south to capture Richmond, Virginia's capital."

Henry explained that the Union needed a victory badly, that people up north were losing faith in their army and their generals. "It seemed like we were sure to win in Fredericksburg."

Except that the rebels knew exactly what the Union was planning. And they were ready.

Henry said that the rebels had a brilliant commander, the general Robert E. Lee. Somehow he always figured out where the Union army was going to be, and how they planned to attack. Sure enough, he had figured out the Union plan to attack Fredericksburg.

"He sent thousands of soldiers into the hills above the town," Henry said. "He also sent dozens of cannons into the hills."

Thomas knew that both sides had these mighty weapons, which were so heavy they had to be pulled by horses, and so powerful they needed at least four men to operate them. Some of the big guns shot cannonballs that were even heavier than Thomas. Others shot shells, explosives that were filled with razor-sharp metal strips, nails, and metal balls. Just one exploding shell could kill ten men in seconds.

"The rebels had the high ground," Henry explained. "Anyone trying to get near those hills was going to get mowed down. And that's exactly what happened."

Henry described how the first Union regiment attacked, how lines of soldiers went charging across a field toward the hills.

"They didn't even get close," he said.

Kaboom!

Kaboom!

Kaboom!

Rebel cannons thundered hundreds of blasts every minute.

And with every blast, Union soldiers fell.

Men who managed to survive the artillery blasts were met with a storm of bullets.

"Within minutes, there were hundreds of our men lying dead and wounded in the mud," Henry said.

But the Union generals wouldn't admit that their plan was a failure.

They sent more regiments out to attack. And every time was the same:

Kaboom!

Kaboom!

Kaboom!

More soldiers dead or wounded, their bodies bleeding and shattered.

"And then it was our turn," Henry said.

Henry's regiment lined up and started charging toward the hills.

"There was so much smoke, we could barely see," he said. "There were bodies everywhere."

Halfway through the charge, Henry's leg seemed to get stuck between two rocks.

He pulled, but it wouldn't come loose.

As the smoke cleared, he saw that it was a fallen Union soldier who had taken hold of his boot, clutching it with all of his might.

Henry thought the man wanted help.

"But he didn't," Henry said. "He knew he was dying. He was trying to stop me from running into that death trap."

Cannons exploded with their deadly fire.

Men fell like stalks of corn cut down by invisible blades.

Henry managed to crawl off the field.

Other men weren't as lucky.

"A hundred and fifty-six of our men died that day," he said. "Over two hundred more were wounded."

Four more regiments were sent in before the generals finally ordered the Union army to retreat.

In all, more than 12,000 soldiers were killed or wounded in Fredericksburg.

Henry looked at Thomas now.

"Our men are worried," he said. "This is our first fight since Fredericksburg. And we need to win it."

All around Thomas, men were lining up to march, their faces grim and scared.

Something terrible was coming.

Thomas could feel it, too.

CHAPTER 9

JULY 2, 1863
THE ROUTE TO GETTYSBURG,
PENNSYLVANIA

They marched two by two along the dusty road, camping at night, and then setting out again before dawn. The days were scorching hot, and some men had collapsed on the side of the road, their faces beet red, their wool uniforms soaked in sweat.

Birdie rode in the wagon with Les and Homer.

But Thomas marched with Henry.

Henry told stories as they walked, about his parents and the store they owned, how his town smelled like apples in the fall, about his sweetheart, Mary. He had shown Thomas and Birdie a picture of Mary, a pretty and serious-looking girl with a thick brown braid. They were both teachers at a little school in their town.

Henry had also shown them his most precious possession: a small book Mary had made for him. It had a tin cover, and was filled with paintings of their town in Vermont. In one of the pictures the trees and grass were covered with what looked like a thick white blanket.

"That's snow," Henry had explained. "It comes from the sky, like tiny icy flowers. There's nothing more beautiful than the first snow in Vermont."

Birdie had closed her eyes and smiled, as if she could see it all in her imagination.

Thomas wished he could. But it seemed his

mind had stopped making happy pictures when Clem was taken.

"I told Mary all about you," Henry said now. "In my last letter."

"You wrote about me?" Thomas said, trying not to smile.

Hearing that made him feel important.

"One day you'll be able to write your own letters," Henry said.

Thomas wondered if Henry was right. He hadn't learned how to read or write; teaching a slave to read was illegal all over the South.

"Clem knew how to read," Thomas said.

Henry always liked hearing about Clem.

"How did he manage to learn?" Henry asked.

"One winter, one of Mr. Knox's sons got sick," Thomas said. "So Mrs. Knox gave him lessons at home. Clem would sneak up to the house, and stand on a bucket outside the window so he could hear."

"That's clever!" Henry said with a laugh.

Thomas remembered how Clem would stay up late into the night. "He'd burn a candle so he could practice scratching letters into the dirt," he told Henry.

Some mornings Thomas woke up and the entire floor of their shack was covered with words, as though Clem had spelled out all of his dreams.

"But then Mr. Knox caught him. He noticed that Clem wasn't in the fields when he was supposed to be, and he found him up at the house, his ear close to the window. He saw all the words written in the dirt."

"What did he do?"

Thomas glanced at Henry.

He hadn't meant to tell this part. He tried never to think about it.

"He whipped him."

Thomas closed his eyes, trying to stop the flood of memories — the *thwack* of Mr. Knox's whip, Clem's shouts of pain, the sight of Clem's blood-soaked shirt.

"Clem couldn't walk for two weeks."

"For learning to read?" Henry said, his eyes blazing with anger and shock.

"Yes, sir," Thomas said.

They marched quietly for a moment, and then Henry turned.

He put his hand on Thomas's arm.

"There are plenty of bad people in the world," he said. "Too many to count. But there are good people, too."

"I know that," Thomas said, looking around at all of the men.

He had found that out over these past two weeks.

Henry seemed to have more to say, but two soldiers appeared on horseback with a message for Captain Campbell.

Tens of thousands of troops were already in Gettysburg. The battle had begun.

"This is it!" the captain bellowed. "To Gettysburg!"

The men raised their rifles and cheered along,

but their eyes looked uncertain. Their words seemed to disappear quickly into the air, like dust.

They'd just started marching again when Henry suddenly turned to Thomas.

"I've been thinking," he said, "that when all this is over, you and Birdie should come live in Vermont. You could go to my school. Mary is a wonderful teacher. She'll have you both reading in no time."

Him and Birdie in Vermont?

With Henry?

Going to school?

"What do you think?"

Thomas smiled, too stunned to speak at first.

And then the soldier marching in front of them fell to the ground. He landed on his back, his eyes gazing blankly up at the sky.

There was a mark on the man's forehead, like the wormhole in an apple, only bigger.

Blood poured from the hole, making a puddle around his head.

The man had been shot dead.

CHAPTER 10

Suddenly the ground was shaking, and hundreds of gray soldiers on horseback poured from the wooded hillside.

"Rebel cavalry!"

"We're under attack!"

Henry grabbed Thomas and dragged him back into the grass, throwing him onto the ground so hard that the air was knocked from his lungs.

"Line up! Line up!" Captain Campbell shouted.

Thomas had watched the men drill back at the camp.

They'd practice for hours, lining up in different battle formations, shooting at targets hundreds of yards away. During drills they sometimes smiled and joked as they marched, tossing their hats into the air and catching them with the sharp metal tips of their bayonets.

This was nothing like the drills.

The men were dead serious. Even those who had been sagging during the march were now moving with lightning speed. With swift motions, the men ripped open their ammunition cartridges with their teeth, poured gunpowder down the barrels of their rifles, then pushed the bullets in with ramrods.

"Stay down, Thomas!" Henry yelled. "Get behind me!"

"Take aim!" the captain screamed.

The soldiers all dropped to one knee, pointing their rifles at the charging cavalrymen.

"Ready! Fire!"

Boom! Boom! Boom! Boom!

Bullets from a hundred muskets tore through the air.

Five rebel soldiers fell from their horses, tumbling onto the ground, rolling down the hill.

"Reload and fire at will!" the captain shouted.

Within seconds, the men had their rifles reloaded.

Boom, boom, boom!

More soldiers fell.

Black gun smoke filled the air, mixing with the dust.

And as quickly as they had appeared, the cavalrymen were gone.

The Union soldiers stood up, catching their breath, running to help the few men who lay on the ground, wincing in pain.

And then suddenly Thomas's mind roared with panic.

Birdie!

He leaped forward, staggering through the smoke.

He managed to find the wagon that Birdie had been riding in. It was tipped over.

Sacks of flour and beans were scattered everywhere, some burst open by bullets.

Lester and Homer were both in the grass, looking dazed and bruised.

"Homer!" Thomas said. "Where's Birdie?"

"Good Lord, I thought she was with you!" Homer said, jumping up. "Lester hurt his leg. I was trying to help him. And with all the smoke . . ."

Thomas looked all around, praying he'd see Birdie running across the field, calling his name.

But she was nowhere to be seen.

Soon dozens of men were looking everywhere for her.

They searched other wagons.

They combed through the tall grass.

Finally Thomas and Henry crossed the road and walked to the edge of the woods.

Something caught Thomas's eye, something small lying on the ground.

It was Birdie's doll.

He picked it up.

It was splattered with blood.

CHAPTER 11

Captain Campbell studied the doll.

Thomas could see the dread in the eyes of the men gathered around them.

"I fear they took her, son," Captain Campbell said. "The rebel cavalry has been kidnapping escaped slaves. Free Negroes, too, all over these parts. They're rounding them up and taking them south to be sold."

Thomas's mind spun. He swayed, and Henry grabbed his elbow to steady him.

"We must do something, sir," said Henry.

Other men murmured in agreement.

"I'm sorry," the captain said. "But there's a battle just ahead. Our orders are to double step it, to get to Gettysburg tonight."

"It won't take us long to find her. . . ." said Henry.

A chorus rose up.

"I'm in!"

"Let's go!"

"Attention!" Captain Campbell shouted.

The men fell silent.

"There is a battle just ahead! We have our orders!"

"Sir," Henry said, glancing at Thomas, "what does this war mean if we turn our backs and let those men carry that little girl away? What are we fighting for, anyway?"

The men seemed to hold their breath, waiting for Captain Campbell to speak.

The captain shook his head.

And that was it for Thomas.

He took off into the woods, ignoring the voices of the men calling after him.

He smashed through bushes, following the trampled path that the horses had made through the brush.

His mind kept flashing back to Clem, to the moment when those men put the chain around his neck.

That could not happen to Birdie!

Thomas heard voices coming from deeper into the woods.

He slowed his steps, and as he came over a small hill he could see them: at least ten men. They were standing around as their horses drank from a rushing stream.

His eyes fell on a sack of flour tied to the saddle of one of the horses.

But then the package lifted its head.

Birdie!

She was looking around. She moved her legs and arms.

Thomas could see no blood on her.

He almost called out but caught himself.

He squinted.

They had tied a rope around her neck.

Anger boiled up inside him.

He wanted to charge at the men.

But he stopped himself. He stood very still.

And then his fury turned to hopelessness.

The men would shoot him before he got anywhere near Birdie.

And even if by some miracle he managed to sneak down and free her, how far could they get?

There was only one choice.

Thomas stood and walked toward the men.

"Thomas!" Birdie shouted, smiling through her tears, as though Thomas could really save her.

Somehow he managed to smile back.

Thomas put his hands up.

"You can take me, too," he said, struggling to keep his voice from breaking, to be strong for Birdie.

He felt the men's hands on him, and he had a strange wilting feeling, as if he was a plant suddenly withering away in the sun.

It was how he'd felt when he was with Mr. Knox — weak and helpless.

A tall rebel soldier strode up to him.

Recognition grabbed Thomas by the throat.

The straggly beard. The cruel glint in his eye.

It was him — the same man who'd beaten Henry, who'd put the pistol to his head, ready to pull the trigger.

He sneered at Thomas. "Well, look here," he said, grabbing Thomas roughly by the arm, squeezing so hard Thomas thought his bone would snap.

A burly man hustled up behind the tall soldier. He had a chest like a barrel and muscles that bulged through his tattered gray jacket.

"This is the one I told you about," sneered the tall man.

He put his face close to Thomas's. His teeth were stained yellow and brown. His breath stunk worse than a dog's.

"Thought you were so smart!" he growled. "I'll show you how smart you are!"

He reached around and took his pistol from his belt.

But the burly man grabbed the tall man's arm and yanked him back hard.

"Easy, soldier," he drawled.

He smiled at Thomas, nodding politely.

He didn't seem cruel. Maybe he'd let them go!

No. He took a rope from his saddlebag and tied Thomas, wrapping his wrists tightly and looping the rope around his neck.

"Don't hurt this one," he said, patting Thomas on the back, as if he was a prized horse. "A strong buck like this? He'll fetch us at least a thousand dollars at the slave auction."

CHAPTER 12

At least the men had not hurt Birdie. She'd lost one of her little front teeth when she fell from the wagon. Her mouth was still bleeding a bit. But otherwise she was all right.

And incredibly, she did not seem scared.

"Don't worry, Thomas," Birdie whispered. "Our men are coming for us."

Thomas didn't have the heart to tell her the truth: that they were on their own.

"All right!" the burly man shouted. "Let's move out of here!"

Thomas felt doomed.

He'd heard about the slave auctions, where they'd be lined up like animals. Buyers would check their teeth and their feet. There was little chance that he and Birdie would be sold to the same owner.

He looked up at the sky, wishing, praying, searching for one last flicker of hope.

And then,

Boom!

A rifle shot echoed through the forest, sending birds flapping wildly out of the trees and bushes.

A familiar voice bellowed.

"Drop your weapons!"

It was Captain Campbell.

Thomas's heart leaped as familiar faces appeared through the trees.

The captain.

Henry.

Homer.

Even Lester was there, though he was hobbling and in obvious pain.

There were at least fifty more Union soldiers with them.

"We have you surrounded," the captain said. "We will shoot every one of you if you don't put your rifles down."

Thomas couldn't imagine how they had managed to sneak into the woods. But they had, and now they had formed an armed circle around the rebels.

The cavalrymen put down their rifles. Captain Campbell stepped forward.

"We have not come here to do battle. We have not come to take prisoners. We have come for the children."

The burly man stepped forward.

"We didn't hurt them," he said. "We didn't lay a hand on them."

Captain Campbell signaled to Henry, who headed for Thomas and Birdie.

The tall man glared at him with narrow eyes.

And then, quick as a flash, he reached behind himself and grabbed something from his belt. His pistol!

He aimed it at Henry.

Boom!

The tall man jerked back, dropped his weapon, and fell to the ground, clutching his leg.

"Anyone else?" the captain shouted, lowering his smoking rifle.

The rebels stood silent, their hands in the air.

Henry grabbed the pistol from the dirt.

He rushed over to the tall man, his eyes flashing with wild fury. He aimed the gun at the man's head. He stood for a moment, his hand steady, the pistol glinting in the sun. Henry looked like a different person, his eyes filled with fury . . . and even hate.

But then he lowered his arm.

"No," he said.

He turned and hurled the pistol into the churning waters of the nearby stream, which swept it away.

Some of the men gasped; Thomas knew how prized those Confederate pistols were, and that some Union soldiers tried to capture them on the battlefields, to bring home as trophies.

But not Henry.

He strode over and cut Thomas and Birdie's ropes with his knife.

Thomas picked up Birdie and held her tight. Her whole body trembled, and she buried her face in his neck.

Henry wrapped a strong arm around Thomas's shoulder, and they walked slowly together toward the road.

Thomas braced himself for more shots.

But they made it to the road, and minutes later, the rest of the soldiers appeared.

They'd captured all of the men's horses and their rifles.

"Those rebs won't be bothering us again," Captain Campbell said.

The rest of the regiment was ahead, and now they'd have to move quickly to catch up. Thomas climbed into the supply wagon with Birdie; he was going to stick close to her from now on.

Before long, she fell asleep on Thomas's shoulder.

Henry and Captain Campbell walked alongside the wagon, their eyes scanning the woods, their rifles loaded and ready.

Thomas kept a grip on Birdie.

It was some time before he stopped shaking, before he could peel his eyes away from the hills. For a few minutes he even managed to sleep.

But soon there was thundering in the distance, and great clouds of black and white smoke billowing in the sky.

At first Thomas thought it was a rainstorm coming toward them.

But no.

"Cannons," Henry said.

It was the Battle of Gettysburg.

And they were heading right for it.

CHAPTER 13

JULY 2, 1863
8:30 P.M.
GETTYSBURG, PENNSYLVANIA

It was getting dark when they arrived. The fighting had ended for the day, and at first, the news about the day's fighting seemed grim: The Union troops had been badly outnumbered. They had lost thousands of soldiers.

But then Captain Campbell learned that somehow, the scrappy Union soldiers had managed to hold the high ground. "Our cannons are in the hills," he said. "We're dug in!"

Troops had been pouring into Gettysburg all day, and tens of thousands more would arrive overnight.

The roads around the town were so crowded that the wagon Thomas and Birdie were riding in could barely move.

They got out and walked with Henry.

Thomas had never seen so many people in one place — thousands of Union soldiers. As they made their way through the town, it seemed that every inch of grass was covered by a tent. Supply wagons lined the roads. Horses and mules were tied to every fence and tree.

Henry talked to some of the soldiers they passed, eager for news of the day's fighting. But these men were just arriving, too. Some men looked more ragged than Birdie's doll. One soldier said his regiment had been marching for more than three weeks.

Birdie stared at the crowds of men.

"They're all here to protect us?" she said, her eyes wide in amazement.

Thomas almost smiled — of course Birdie would think that this was her own personal army.

Henry picked Birdie up. "Yes, Bird," he said. "They are here for you."

Thomas could see Henry wasn't joking.

And maybe Birdie wasn't wrong.

These men *were* fighting for him and Birdie, weren't they?

Fighting so that they could be free.

Henry carried Birdie as they passed a long line of supply wagons stuck on the side of the road.

Suddenly Birdie gasped.

"Look at those men!" she cried, pointing.

Thomas turned, and he too stared at the crowd of men surrounding the front wagon.

"They look like us!" Birdie exclaimed.

The men were black.

"They're teamsters," Henry said. "They're paid by the Union army to run supplies from camp

to camp. It's tough work. Dangerous, too. We've got thousands of those men working for us. We couldn't fight this war without them."

Thomas felt a jolt of excitement.

Those men were free! They were working for the Union!

"Hello!" Birdie sang out as they passed, waving madly. "Hello!"

The men looked up in surprise, their tired and dusty faces melting into smiles at the sight of Birdie.

Thomas wished he could talk to them. Where had they come from? How had they gotten here?

But there was no time. Their regiment had been ordered to set up camp in a wooded field outside of the town and wait for their orders.

"We're in for a tough battle tomorrow," Captain Campbell said. "Get rest now, but be ready, men."

The men dropped their bedrolls and knapsacks and collapsed to the ground. They peeled off their boots and socks and washed their bloodied and blistered feet. And then most of them fell asleep, not even bothering to eat supper or spread out their blankets.

Thomas and Birdie slept, too.

But sometime later that night, the entire camp was awakened by the bugler, followed by Captain Campbell's booming voice.

"Wake up, men!" he bellowed. "The time has come!"

The men staggered to their feet and gathered around the captain.

"We will march across the ridge and take up a position in the hills," the captain announced, pointing into the darkness behind them. "By morning, the rebels will be on the attack. Our mission is to help hold the ground."

Just hours ago the men had looked so ragged and battered they could barely stand. Now they were alert, standing strong.

"The fighting will be fierce," the captain said. "The rebels will come at us hard. They will fight with all of their might to knock us from those hills, to crush us. But we will hold our ground, men! We will hold our ground!"

The soldiers listened with hard expressions.

"Yes, Captain!" a soldier yelled.

"We will hold the ground!" shouted another.

The captain looked around, his steely gaze seeming to fall on each and every man.

"This is it, men," he said, his voice rising. "Everything has led to this place, to this moment! This is our time!"

Someone shouted out a word:

"*Fredericksburg!*"

It seemed to hover there in the air.

Someone else shouted it out, and then more and more, until the shouts were a wild chanting chorus.

"*Fredericksburg!*"

"*Fredericksburg!*"

"*Fredericksburg!*"

The men pumped their fists, their eyes fiery.

And at first Thomas didn't understand.

Why would they want to remember that terrible battle, where their regiment had lost so many men? Were they thinking they would lose this battle, too?

But as the chants grew louder, Thomas could see that the men were turning that day into something new, something strong that they would take with them into battle.

Finally the captain held up his hands.

"Let's go, men!"

As the men scrambled to line up, Henry took Thomas aside.

"You and Birdie will stay here with Homer and Les," he said. "They will keep you safe. You will stay with them, no matter what."

Thomas nodded.

A man shouted to Henry, "Come on!"

Henry ignored him.

He put his hands on Thomas's shoulders. And he looked him straight in the eye.

"Remember what I told you," he said. "During the march. That I want you and Birdie to come to Vermont."

"We will go," Thomas said. "We want to go with you."

"Good," Henry said. "You will have a fine and happy life there."

"I know we will," Thomas said.

Captain Campbell was yelling now, ordering the men to start marching.

"And, Thomas, we can't know what will happen out there. So I want you to make me a promise."

He gripped Thomas tighter.

"No matter what happens to me, you will go to Vermont. You will live with my family."

What was Henry saying?

"Promise me," Henry said, his eyes fixed on Thomas's.

Thomas nodded weakly.

Henry reached into his knapsack, and pulled out the book of paintings Mary had made for him.

"Keep this for me," he said, slipping it into Thomas's shirt pocket.

Then he put his hand on Thomas's head, nodded, and quickly turned away.

A second later he was gone.

CHAPTER 14

When the fighting began, explosions of cannon fire were booming from both sides.

The explosions got louder and louder, and came so quickly that there was just one tremendous noise, as though every tree on earth was crashing to the ground at once.

The earth under their feet shook.

The noise pounded in their ears.

Birdie stayed in the wagon with Les, whose leg was in such bad shape that he could barely walk. Homer and Thomas stood on a big rock near the wagon. They could see the hills and the fields below. Right now, there was too much cannon smoke to see much.

But earlier that morning, when all was still quiet, Homer had pointed out the spot where the men from their regiment were positioned: a small hill covered with scrubby trees and big rocks. It didn't look like much, especially from far away. But it was one of the highest points in Gettysburg. "It's worth fighting for," Homer said. "And our men are tough. By God, we'll fight for it. If those rebels want it, they're going to have to try to rip it out of our hands."

He'd pointed to the meadow, just below the rocky hill.

"I'd guess that, within a few hours, there are going to be thousands of rebel troops charging across that meadow to try to take the high ground."

Thomas kept his eye on the smoky scene below. Every so often a gust of wind would clear the smoke for a few seconds, and Thomas would catch a glimpse of the field.

So far there were no soldiers charging across it. Maybe there never would be.

Suddenly a messenger on horseback came galloping up.

"The captain needs the ammunition wagon right away!"

"We were ordered to stay here," Homer said.

"They need more cartridges now!"

"All right," Homer said. "We'll get it right up there."

Les got up and tried to hop over to the ammunition wagon, his face sweaty and white with pain.

"Let me go," Thomas said.

Birdie was fast asleep. He would be back before she woke up.

Homer and Les looked nervously at each other, but then Homer gave a nod.

Thomas hopped onto the wagon, and Homer snapped the reins. The horses moved swiftly, out of the field and up a dusty road.

"Keep your head down," Homer said.

The horses faltered, struggling to get up a rocky stretch of the road.

They'd barely made it to the top of the hill when there was a whistling sound.

"Look out!" a voice screamed.

There was a deafening explosion.

Kaboom!

And a tree right behind them shattered into a million shards of wood.

The horses panicked, and Homer quickly unhitched them from the wagon.

"Come on!" he called. "Let's grab some boxes and run up there!"

But then there was more whistling. . . .

"Thomas! Run!"

Thomas sprinted away seconds before a cannonball smashed into the wagon.

Kabooooooom!

Thomas felt as though his head had been smacked into a stone wall. A shard of metal sliced his forehead. Another carved a jagged gash into his right thigh.

The wagon erupted into a fireball as he hit the ground. Flames chased after him. Men groaned and screamed.

"Thomas!" called Homer.

Thomas gasped in the smoke. Blood spilled into his eyes. He couldn't breathe. Burning wood surrounded him.

He crawled away, his leg throbbing with pain. He was desperate to escape the flames and smoke.

He rolled down the hill, down, down, down, until he reached the flat grass of the meadow.

His head pounded. He could feel the blood gushing from his leg. It was a bad cut. Very bad.

The smoke burned his eyes and his lungs. It was hard to breathe, to even think.

Down in the grass, there wasn't as much smoke. A breeze blew and for a few seconds the air cleared. Thomas could see across the field.

He froze in terror.

There they were, rebel soldiers ready to charge. There were thousands of them — men in front on horseback, waving gleaming swords. Behind them, two lines of men stretched across the entire meadow, soldiers with their rifles raised.

Suddenly there was a noise, rising above the booms, a howling scream that rushed across the meadow like a raging wind.

The rebel yell.

The men were screaming as they began their charge across the meadow.

Thomas had to get away. But where could he go?

The rebel cannons still boomed, sending their deadly balls and shells into the hills behind him. Thomas turned to climb back up to the high ground.

But now there was the thundering of thousands of pounding rebel boots.

It was too late. A rebel soldier was running toward Thomas, his eyes glowing bloodred through the smoke, his face twisted into an awful killing grin.

"No!" Thomas screamed.

He couldn't die here.

He couldn't leave Birdie!

Boom!

The bullet hit Thomas, and his chest seemed to explode.

The world around him spun. The sky fell, and the air turned bright white.

Thomas hit the ground hard, his body sinking into soft, blood-soaked grass.

CHAPTER 15

Later, there was pain.

And voices calling to him.

Was he dead?

No, he was back with Mr. Knox.

That must be why his entire body hurt. Because he was back on the farm, working dawn to dusk.

He could hear Birdie, feel her little hand gripping his.

But who was that other man calling his name?

"Thomas!"

"Thomas!"

Thomas tried to open his eyes, but there was just darkness.

He tried to speak, but his voice was like ashes.

He wanted to move, but he felt hands holding him down.

Or were they chains?

Searing pain ripped across his chest.

Mr. Knox! Please don't whip me!

He was a slave again.

Or was he dead?

Two days passed before Thomas realized that he was alive, and that he was not back at Mr. Knox's farm.

He was in a hospital tent, still in Gettysburg.

He'd been carried off the battlefield along with thousands of others. His pants had been soaked in blood. His eyes were swollen shut.

When the ambulance crew was searching the field for wounded, at first they thought Thomas was dead. But then they heard him shout.

"Birdie!"

They had put him on a stretcher carefully, wondering how on earth this boy had gotten himself onto this battlefield, assuming he was a servant to one of the officers.

Most of his blood had spilled into the grass, from the enormous gash on his leg.

The rebel's bullet had bruised his chest.

It would have killed him, ripped right through his heart.

Except it was stopped by the tin-covered book in his shirt pocket.

Mary's book of paintings.

That's what saved his life. Not a rifle or a sword.

He was saved by a book filled with pretty pictures of a world Thomas had never seen.

The doctors stitched him up and left him, caught between life and death, as battles raged all around Gettysburg. They fought for three days in all. They battled in meadows and fields, in orchards and woods, on hilltops and in valleys. Streams ran red with blood. Twenty-three thousand men were killed or wounded before the rebels finally retreated.

The Union troops held their high ground.

But Thomas knew none of this.

He didn't know that Homer was killed by a shell.

And that Captain Campbell was brought down as he tried to protect two of his men from charging rebel soldiers.

And that Henry was hit by a bullet, which shattered his leg.

Thomas learned all this days later, when his head finally cleared.

And in that first moment after he opened his eyes, he thought he was dreaming, or in Heaven.

Because there was Birdie, smiling at him through tears.

And next to her was the man who'd been calling Thomas's name:

Clem.

CHAPTER 16

NOVEMBER 8, 1863
BURLINGTON, VERMONT

Thomas sat at a desk next to Birdie, carefully writing out his letters.

All around the schoolroom, children sat quietly as their pretty teacher watched over them. Every so often she came to Thomas's desk.

"Fine work, Thomas," said Miss Ashford — Mary.

Henry's sweetheart.

Thomas nodded, hoping he didn't look too proud. It had been five months since they arrived, and his handwriting was looking better. He practiced for hours every night, sitting at Henry's old desk as Mr. and Mrs. Green sat nearby and read. Henry's parents still weren't sleeping much, and they seemed glad to have a reason to keep their candles burning into the night.

"Look at mine, Miss Ashford!" Birdie said, holding up her paper, covered with wobbly letters.

Miss Ashford smiled at Birdie, then put her finger in front of her lip with a gentle shush.

Birdie loved school more than anyone, but she kept forgetting she wasn't the only student.

At lunchtime Thomas and Birdie sat under a tree. It was getting colder, and the sky was gray. Soon winter would come. Mrs. Green had already sewn three wool dresses for Birdie, and two new pairs of trousers for Thomas.

Thomas ate his lunch and looked around the schoolyard. The air smelled like apples.

Just like Henry had said.

Thomas swallowed hard, and glanced at Birdie.

She didn't have to ask him why he was sad.

No, Henry hadn't made it.

But they had come here to Vermont, like he told them to, and his family had welcomed them, just like he promised they would. The whole town did.

Thomas had been shocked to see the stacks of letters Henry had written, pages filled with stories about Thomas and Birdie.

"What a gift to have you here with us," Mrs. Green had said when they first arrived. "A gift from Henry."

It was Clem who'd brought them here, on the train, one month after Gettysburg. During that long ride Clem had told them every detail of what had happened to him after he was taken away from Mr. Knox's. The plantation in Mississippi had been a brutal place, where slaves were worked to the bone picking cotton in the blistering sun. After a year, Clem escaped.

He'd traveled more than six hundred miles on his own, dodging snakes and bears and slave catchers. "I was coming to get you both," he said. "I wanted us to go north together."

But in North Carolina, he was caught by a band of rebel soldiers, taken just like Birdie. They got him halfway back to Mississippi when he was freed by a band of teamsters, who attacked the rebel camp at night and helped Clem and four other men escape.

Clem went to work with them, running wagon trains filled with supplies.

After Gettysburg, Clem had loved being in Vermont with Thomas, Birdie, and Mr. and Mrs. Green.

But he could only stay one week before he headed back down south. Mr. and Mrs. Green wanted him to stay longer, but Clem had a new plan: to be a soldier for the North. He had already signed up to be in one of the first black regiments of the Union army.

"I'll be back here," Clem had said as he'd hugged them all good-bye. "I promise I'll be back when it's all done."

He wrote to them almost every day now, and Thomas would sit for hours sounding out every word. He could hear Clem's voice in his mind, describing the battles, the people he met, his plans for after the war.

"We'll be together," he wrote. *"Can you picture it?"*

And Thomas could.

His mind was *filled* with bright pictures now.

At first, most of the pictures had appeared in his nightmares: the wagon in flames, the vultures that had circled above the battlefield as he lay wounded, the glowing red eyes of the rebel who shot him.

But there were happier pictures, too: the memories of Birdie and Clem standing by his bed in the hospital tent, of Mr. and Mrs. Green waiting for them at the train station.

And now, in the schoolyard, he closed his eyes, and he saw the newest pictures, the pictures of his hopes: that this terrible war would end; that Clem would be back with them soon; that they would be here, together and free.

His eyes were still closed when he felt something cold on his cheeks.

He looked up and saw white flakes drifting in the air.

"Thomas!" Birdie cried. "It's snow!"

Thomas put his arms around his little sister.

And together they watched the icy flowers fall from the sky.

A TRIP BACK IN TIME

Each I Survived book takes me on a trip back in time. Sometimes I get so deep into my research that I imagine I really am in the midst of events that happened decades or even centuries ago.

I've "traveled" to some frightening moments as the author of this series — to the decks of the *Titanic* as it was sinking, to a creek invaded by a man-eating shark, to the shores of Hawaii as bombs rained down on Pearl Harbor.

But I don't think there is a darker or more

frightening time in American history than the Civil War.

During those four long years, Americans were fighting against other Americans. Our nation came incredibly close to being torn in two. Beautiful cities of the South were burned to the ground. And thousands of soldiers died every month. Nobody knows exactly how many people died during the war, but historians estimate that it was about 750,000. That's more than the number who died in all of the other wars America has fought combined. Almost every American lost somebody in the Civil War.

And even before the war began, there was slavery. By 1860, nearly four million people were slaves. They were men like your father, women like your mom and me, kids like you. Can you imagine what it would be like to be owned by another person, to be treated like a dog or a horse, to have no say in what happened to you?

To try to understand this time in history, I read thirty-one books — histories, diaries, novels, biographies, and autobiographies. I studied maps, watched movies, stared at photographs taken 150 years ago.

I also visited Gettysburg, Pennsylvania, with my husband and our two youngest kids, Dylan and Valerie. If you go there — and I hope you can — you will think it is one of the prettiest places you've ever seen, a charming little town surrounded by green rolling hills, sweeping meadows, and quiet forests.

We toured the battlefields and visited its amazing museum. Afterward, we climbed up to Little Round Top. This is the rocky hill where some of the fiercest fighting took place.

As my own children climbed on huge boulders and my husband took pictures, I looked out on the meadow below and imagined how it must have looked in July of 1863. There were thousands and thousands of dead bodies in the grass by the last day, each one someone's son or husband or brother or best friend. If we had been alive in 1863, my two oldest sons — who are now nineteen and twenty-two years old — would have been soldiers in the war, and it's likely they would have been a part of this battle with one of the Connecticut regiments that fought there.

As I stood there, I thought of the words of a young Confederate soldier in one of the histories I read. He had written a letter to his sister back home in Alabama, sent from Gettysburg just after the final rebel charge.

"I ask myself," he wrote, *"if many years from now, anyone will remember what happened here, if they will ever think of those who were lost."*

Yes, I wanted to tell him. We remember.

QUESTIONS AND ANSWERS ABOUT THE CIVIL WAR, AND MORE

The Civil War lasted for four years, 1861–1865. It is a huge and fascinating subject, and I learned so much while researching and writing this book. I wish we could spend about a month together so I could tell you everything I discovered. But I know you're very busy. So here are answers to a few questions I thought might be on your mind.

Is the story of Thomas and Birdie true?
All of the books in my I Survived series are historical fiction. That means that the facts are

all true — the dates, the settings, the names of generals and presidents. But the characters come from my imagination, inspired by details I discover from my research.

Thomas and Birdie were not real people. But everything that happened to them really did happen to other kids — they were slaves, they weren't allowed to learn to read or write, their family members were sold, they escaped and found safety with Union troops.

Thousands of slaves attempted to escape from the South. They followed the North Star. They braved terror and hunger. Most died on their journeys or were captured by slave hunters and brought back to their owners.

But some succeeded, such as Harriet Tubman, who escaped and then returned to the South over and over to lead others to freedom. Her story and those of others like her are unforgettable and far more thrilling than any stories I could ever make up.

What caused the Civil War?

This is the most complicated question of all, and people have written whole books explaining it. But here's the simplest answer: The war was about slavery.

Remember, America was supposed to be "land of the free."

Think of the words in our Declaration of Independence, "all men are created equal."

These words are at the very heart of what America was supposed to be.

And yet by 1860, four million people in the South were slaves. That makes no sense, right?

No, it doesn't. Many things in history are almost impossible to understand when we look back on them. Even smart people we admire had beliefs that we can't understand today. They did things that we now know are wrong and shameful.

Owning slaves is one of those things.

But sadly, slavery has been a fact of human life for thousands of years. In America, before the first Europeans arrived, Native American tribes kept slaves captured during wars and raids. When the European settlers arrived here, they brought slaves to do hard work.

George Washington owned slaves. So did Thomas Jefferson.

But over time, ideas about slavery changed. People came to see that it was evil and wrong. When Abraham Lincoln became president, more and more people in the North were saying that America should not have slavery anywhere. Already it was illegal in the North. They said it had to be banned in the South, too.

There were big fights about this. For many people in the South, slaves were their most valuable possessions. A strong young slave like Thomas was worth at least one thousand dollars, which is more than it cost to buy a large home. On big farms known as plantations, owners depended on hundreds of slaves to do the back-breaking work in the fields. If slavery became illegal, these plantation owners would have to pay people to do the work. The slave owners were sure they would go out of business.

People in the North and South argued about slavery for years. Finally, leaders of eleven Southern states decided that they didn't want to be a part of America anymore. In 1861, these states "seceded" and became their own country, known as the Confederate States of America. President Lincoln couldn't let that happen. He believed that keeping our country together was a cause worth fighting for.

Do you agree?

Why was the Battle of Gettysburg so important?

There were many terrible and bloody battles during the Civil War. You might have heard the names of some of them: Bull Run, Antietam, and the Battle of the Wilderness. Gettysburg was the bloodiest of all. More men were lost there than in any other battle. ("Lost" means soldiers who were killed, wounded, captured, or missing.)

But there's more to Gettysburg than death and destruction. The Battle of Gettysburg "changed the tide" of the war. That means that before Gettysburg, the war was heading one way — the South was winning. After Gettysburg, they no longer were.

In the year before Gettysburg, the Southern troops had won every major battle except for one, Antietam. Many people, including powerful people in the North, said the Union should give up. They were losing faith in President Abraham Lincoln. An election was coming up. Most people predicted that he wouldn't win.

Gettysburg changed that. The Union victory at Gettysburg gave people in the North the will to keep fighting — and the belief that they could win. President Abraham Lincoln was reelected. He vowed not to give up the fight.

For people in the South, the loss was devastating. They lost 28,000 men during those three days, more than a third of their army. The North lost 23,000, but their army was bigger, and there were more people living in the North. So there were always new soldiers to take the place of those who had died.

The war didn't end with Gettysburg — far from it. It dragged on for two more years. Thousands and thousands more soldiers died. Southern cities were burned to the ground.

But the Union did finally win. And many say that the road to victory began at Gettysburg.

And some last (very important) words
Before I say good-bye to you, I'd like to take you with me on one last trip back to the time of the Civil War. So close your eyes, and let's travel back to November 19, 1863, to Gettysburg, Pennsylvania.

It's a cold and dreary day. We've taken a train to Gettysburg because we want to attend a special ceremony in honor of a new cemetery. More than four thousand Union soldiers are buried there, all killed on the Gettysburg battlefield. We listen to a speech by a man named Edward Everett, a former president of Harvard University.

He speaks for more than two hours. And though he's a great speaker, we are probably eager to leave when he's done.

But then a second speaker gets up. He is extremely tall — a foot taller than the average man in those days. It is our president, Abraham Lincoln. The war has taken a terrible toll on him. His face is worn and tired. But his eyes are bright with intelligence, goodness, and bravery.

And he is indeed a very smart, honest, and courageous man.

He speaks for only two minutes. His message is clear: that the war is about nothing less than the very survival of America. And that to honor the men buried in this cemetery, we must not give up fighting for the cause they gave their lives for.

The speech is so short, and the words are so simple, that most people don't even clap. Few think it's a good speech.

And it wasn't a good speech. It was an incredible speech. Today, the Gettysburg Address, as it's known, is considered one of the greatest speeches in American history. Read it now. You'll probably want your mom or dad or teacher to read it with you the first time, since some of the language is old-fashioned. But after you read it a few times, you'll understand it very well, and you'll understand what the terrible Civil War meant to our country.

The Gettysburg Address

Four score and seven years ago our fathers brought forth on this continent a new nation, conceived in liberty, and dedicated to the proposition that all men are created equal.

Now we are engaged in a great civil war, testing whether that nation or any nation so conceived and so dedicated can long endure. We are met on a great battlefield of that war. We have come to dedicate a portion of that field as a final resting place for those who here gave their lives that that nation might live.

It is altogether fitting and proper that we should do this.

But, in a larger sense, we can not dedicate, we can not consecrate, we can not hallow this ground. The brave men, living and dead who struggled here, have consecrated it far above our poor power to add or detract. The world will little note, nor long remember what we say here, but it can never forget what they did here. It is for us the living rather to be dedicated here to the unfinished work which they who fought here have thus far so nobly advanced. It is rather for us to be here dedicated to the great task remaining before us — that from these honored dead we take increased devotion to that cause for which they gave the last full measure of devotion — that we here highly resolve that these dead shall not have died in vain, that this nation under God shall have a new birth of freedom, and that government of the people, by the people, for the people shall not perish from the earth.

FOR FURTHER READING

There are tens of thousands of books about the Civil War and slavery. Here are a few that I discovered in my research, and that you might like to read.

A History of US: War, Terrible War 1855-1865, Book Six, by Joy Hakim, Oxford University Press, 2007
There's no better writer of history than Joy Hakim. This is part of her ten-volume American

history series, and I swear you won't even realize you're learning. Everything you need to understand about the Civil War is here as well as an amazing story about General Lee's sword (you need to read the book to find out).

The Long Road to Gettysburg, by Jim Murphy, Sandpiper, 2000

The author uses the real words of soldiers to tell the story of Gettysburg. There are real pictures, too. You'll get a very clear sense of what it was like for the soldiers fighting.

The Boys' War: Confederate and Union Soldiers Talk About the Civil War, by Jim Murphy, Sandpiper, reissue 1993

Many boys and young men fought in the Civil War. Like *The Long Road to Gettysburg*, this book uses the story of real soldiers to show what life was really like for them.

Lincoln: A Photobiography, by
Russell Freedman, Sandpiper, 1989
A fascinating look at one of our greatest presidents.

Elijah of Buxton, by Christopher
Paul Curtis, Scholastic Inc., 2007
This is a novel, but it will give you a clear idea of
what slavery was like in the years just before the
Civil War.

*Moses: When Harriet Tubman Led Her
People to Freedom*, by Carole Boston
Weatherford, illustrated by Kadir
Nelson, Jump at the Sun/Hyperion
Books, 2006
This is a picture book, but it's my favorite about
Harriet Tubman, who escaped from slavery and
then went back to the South to lead others to
freedom.

I SURVIVED

THE ATTACKS OF SEPTEMBER 11, 2001

A DAY THAT WILL CHANGE THE NATION...

The only thing Lucas loves more than football is his dad's friend Benny, a firefighter and former football star. He taught Lucas the game and helps him practice. So when Lucas's parents decide football is too dangerous and he needs to quit, Lucas *has* to talk to his biggest fan.

On a whim, Lucas takes the train to the city instead of the bus to school. It's a bright, beautiful day in New York. But just as Lucas arrives at the firehouse, everything changes . . . and nothing will ever be the same again.